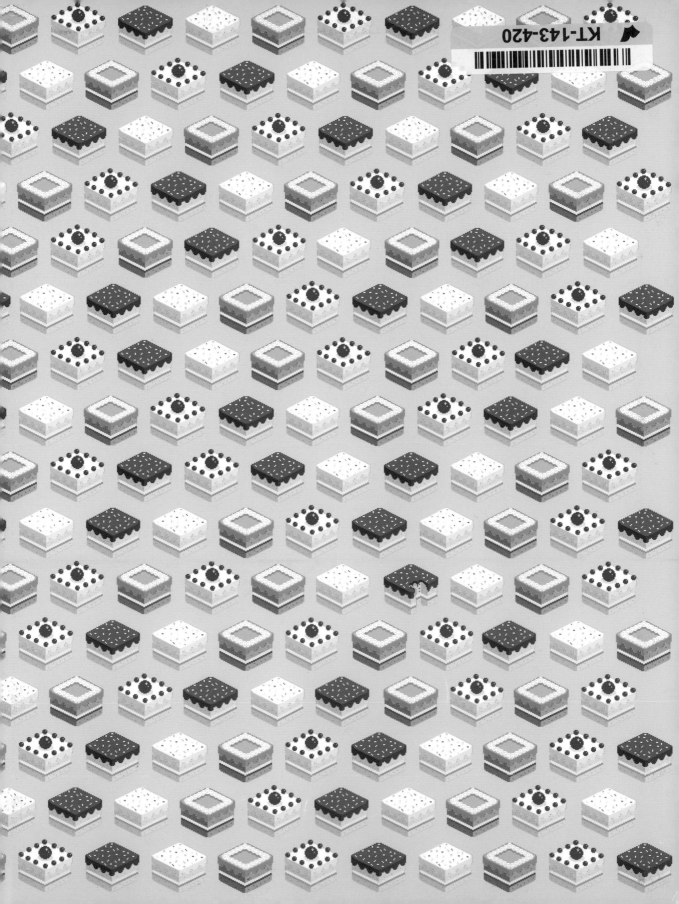

Dedicated to my mum and dad.
Without their support, none
of this would have happened.

EGMONT
We bring stories to life

First published in Great Britain in 2015 by Egmont UK Limited,
The Yellow Building, 1 Nicholas Road, London, W11 4AN

Written by Joseph Garrett.
Illustrations by Adam Murphy, Lisa Murphy, Army of Trolls and Anthony Duke.
Shutterstock.com: Hand drawn business icons set: Lantica,
Socks pixel art: Saphatthachat Sunchoote, 3D cow pixelate isometric vector : maraga,
3D goat pixelate isometric vector : maraga, 3D pig pixelate isometric vector : maraga
3D rat pixelate isometric vector : maraga, Chalkboard: Akura Yochi, Pixel fruits: Miaynata,
Colour pixel art: Polovinkin, Vector abstract design: yoolarts,
Back to school chalkboard doodles: hugolacasse, 36 load indicators set: iconizer.
Photography by Laura Ashman.
Edited by Stephanie Milton.
Designed by Bhavini Jolapara, Tiffany Leeson and Anthony Duke.
Our thanks to Pedro Badla, Poppy Burnham, Bethan Hawes, Alex James and Katie Westlake.

© 2015 Joseph Garrett.

ISBN 978 1 4052 8156 0
63181/20
Printed in Italy

Parental guidance is advised for all craft and colouring activities. Always ask an adult to help when using glue, paint,
scissors, knives and other kitchen equipment. Wear protective clothing and cover surfaces to avoid staining.

**Although the recipe in this book has been specially selected and tested to be used by children,
adult supervision is always necessary when a child is cooking or using sharp implements.**

ONLINE SAFETY FOR YOUNGER FANS
Spending time online is great fun!
Here are a few simple rules to help younger fans stay safe and keep
the internet a great place to spend time:

- Never give out your real name – don't use it as your username.
- Never give out any of your personal details.
- Never tell anybody which school you go to or how old you are.
- Never tell anybody your password except a parent or a guardian.
- Be aware that you must be 13 or over to create an account on many sites.
- Always check the site policy and ask a parent or guardian for permission before registering.
- Always tell a parent or guardian if something is worrying you.

Stay safe online. Any website addresses listed in this book are correct
at the time of going to print. However, Egmont is not responsible for content hosted by third parties.
Please be aware that online content can be subject to change and websites can contain content
that is unsuitable for children. We advise that all children are supervised when using the internet.

The publishers have used every endeavour to secure appropriate permissions for materials reproduced in the book.
In case of any unintentional omission, the publishers will be pleased to hear from the relevant party.

STAMPY'S
LOVELY BOOK

CONTENTS

HELLO!

Welcome to My Lovely Book!

My Lovely World is full of friends, fun and, of course, cake. Now I want to share it all with you so I've filled this book full of games, activities, a cake bake (of course!), lots of secrets about me and my friends, and my best video-making tips so you can create videos like me. **Enjoy!**

www.youtube.com/stampylonghead

8

THIS IS STAMPY

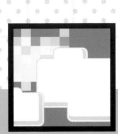

Stampy Cat

DISTINGUISHING FEATURES: Long tail, orange fur, big, fluffy whiskers!

LIKES: Playing games, building and cake.

DISLIKES: Googlies, difficult redstone.

FAVOURITE GAMES: Minecraft, Halo, Disney Infinity, Skylanders.

BEST LOVELY WORLD MOMENT: Finding my first dog.

MOST LIKELY TO SAY: Spruce!

ALL ABOUT ME!

Gosh, aren't these infographics lovely? Take a closer look and you'll learn lots of things about me!

DOGS I'VE OWNED AND THE NUMBER THAT HAVE DIED

OWNED
25

NO LONGER WITH US
14

MY LOVELY FANS AROUND THE WORLD

50%
USA

5.3%
Canada

25%
Uk

13.1%
Other

4.7%
Australia

1.9%
Philippines

MY NEW SUBSCRIBERS PER MONTH [2014-2015]

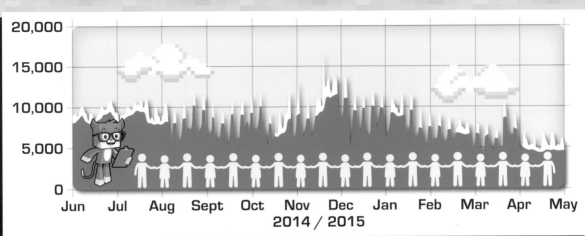

MY HAPPINESS IN RELATION TO THE AMOUNT OF CAKE I'VE CONSUMED

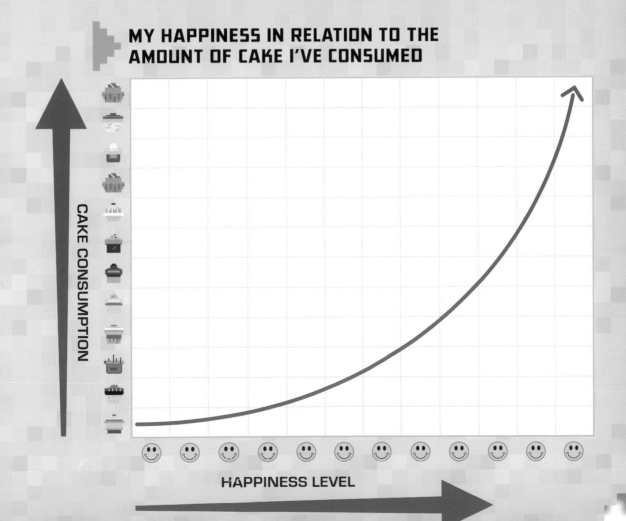

MY FAVOURITE FRIENDS

My Lovely World would have been a lot less lovely
if I hadn't had such amazing friends to share it with.
And my best friends are going to join me in My Lovely Book!
Here's a little bit more about my favourite people:

Ballistic Squid

DISTINGUISHING FEATURES: Big mouth and teeth, blue skin.

HOW WE MET: We met through YouTube.

WHY WE'RE FRIENDS: I am friends with
Squid because he makes me laugh more than
anyone else.

LIKES: Parkour.

DISLIKES: Mazes.

BEST LOVELY WORLD MOMENT:
Being the Kraken in episode 124.

MOST LIKELY TO SAY:

Poop Attack!

Amy Lee 33

DISTINGUISHING FEATURES:
Bright pink hair and is usually seen holding a lovely jubbly love love petal.

HOW WE MET: We met through Xbox!

WHY WE'RE FRIENDS: I always make Amy laugh!

LIKES: Flowers, animals, unicorns and fairies.

DISLIKES: The witch!

BEST LOVELY WORLD MOMENT: Teaching me how to care for flowers in the cool school.

MOST LIKELY TO SAY: *Loves it!*

Rosie

DISTINGUISHING FEATURES: Long, thin beak, orange chest feathers.

HOW WE MET: We met when playing Xbox together in 2008.

WHY WE'RE FRIENDS: We have fun playing lots of different games.

LIKES: Eating fish.

DISLIKES: Hot places.

BEST LOVELY WORLD MOMENT: Riding pigs in my Road Hog game.

MOST LIKELY TO SAY: peckerhead.

MY FAVOURITE FRIENDS 1.

Finnball

DISTINGUISHING FEATURES: Golden crown, black cape, purple uniform.

HOW WE MET: He and his children made a special video to celebrate me getting 10,000 subscribers. Check out 'Happy 10,000 subs Stampy!' on Finnball's YouTube channel!

WHY WE'RE FRIENDS: He is one of the kindest people I know.

LIKES: Playing video games.

DISLIKES: Being beaten by his kids.

BEST LOVELY WORLD MOMENT: His honeymoon with his queen, Lily.

MOST LIKELY TO SAY:

UNTIL NEXT SLIME.

Sqaishey

DISTINGUISHING FEATURES: Fluffy feathers.

HOW WE MET: She made me a puzzle map to play through.

WHY WE'RE FRIENDS: We became friends playing and recording Minecraft together.

LIKES: Having fun and Numming Seeds!

DISLIKES: Falling off things.

BEST LOVELY WORLD MOMENT: Looking after Stampy's pets while he builds.

MOST LIKELY TO SAY:

Meanie Beanies!

LOVE GARDEN ART

I get lots of lovely drawings and artwork from my lovely fans, and the best ones get the honour of appearing in my Love Garden. Here are some of the best fan art pics I've seen!

BRIANNA_LAMBERT

NELLY_NALLY_NELLY

Happy Birthday Stampy

RAIDER_WOLF

Back to School

CARWYN

carwyn

LOVE GARDEN CRAFTS

As well as art, my fans also send me photos of their Stampy-themed craft projects. Here are some of the most creative ways that people have made me!

Madi

Serena

Ken

REMEMBER THE NUMBER ONE RULE: DON'T ASK TO BE ADDED TO THE LOVE GARDEN.

"BUT SERIOUSLY, JUST BETWEEN US, HOW DO I GET MYSELF ADDED TO STAMPY'S LOVE GARDEN?"

This is a question I get asked a lot! The answer is,

DO SOMETHING: o **FUN**
o **CREATIVE**
o **ORIGINAL!**

Catrin

Eleanor

Why not make your own Stampy creation for my Love Garden?

LOST DOGS SEARCH AND FIND

Oh, no! My dogs have escaped from the dog house and have wandered off! Can you help me find them?

My lovely dogs – please find!

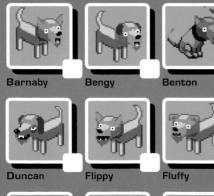

Barnaby   Bengy   Benton

Duncan   Flippy   Fluffy

Gregory Jr   Luna   Sherbet

WOULD YOU RATHER?

Ooh! I've been challenged to a particularly tricky game of Would You Rather?
I've done my best to answer each question. Check out my answers, then maybe you'd like to have a go yourself?

Would you rather kiss a pig or a cow?

I would rather

....

 Stampy says:

A cow!

....

22

Would you rather have a bath full of baked beans or porridge?

I would rather

. . . .

. . . .

Stampy says:

A bath full of baked beans!

. . . .

Would you rather be twice your height or half your height?

I would rather

. . . .

. . . .

Stampy says:

Half my height!

. . . .

Would you rather have whiskers or a tail?

I would rather

. . . .

Stampy says:

A tail please!
. . . .

Would you rather marry a lemon or a lime?

I would rather

. . . .

Stampy says:

Definitely a lime.

. . . .

OTHER ADVENTURES

I'm well known for my fun adventures in Minecraft, but did you know I've had lots of other adventures in other worlds, too? Here are some of the most exciting!

TERRARIA

I built my room inside a tree that is inside a tree!

DISNEY INFINITY

I battled under a giant model of my face in Disney Infinity.

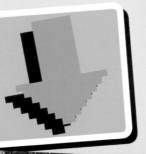

DOKI-DOKI UNIVERSE
I travelled across the galaxy on a piece of cheese!

SKYLANDERS
I captured the Golden Queen in Skylanders: Trap Team.

THE UNFINISHED SWAN
I finished painting the swan in The Unfinished Swan.

PAINFUL PUNS

Sometimes, when I'm making videos, I like to make jokes. Sometimes my jokes are really **punny**. And sometimes my jokes are really, really bad.

Rate my painful puns, from not so bad to really painful by colouring in the number of segments you think each one deserves!

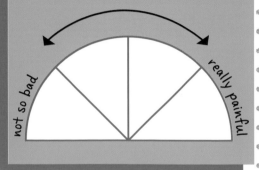

My Stampy puns are cat-astrophic. Sqaishey, quickly – duck!

not so bad · really painful

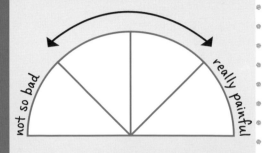

Sorry for milking the cow jokes, I will tell some udder jokes now.

not so bad · really painful

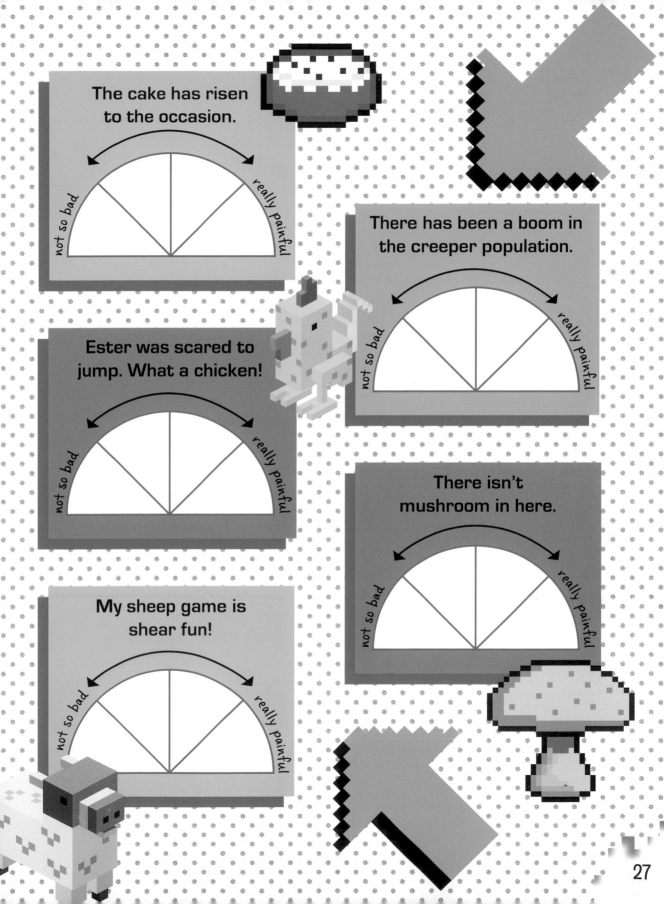

The cake has risen to the occasion.

not so bad — really painful

There has been a boom in the creeper population.

not so bad — really painful

Ester was scared to jump. What a chicken!

not so bad — really painful

There isn't mushroom in here.

not so bad — really painful

My sheep game is shear fun!

not so bad — really painful

27

Having a break from screen time? Stuck for ideas to keep you entertained? Try my anti-boredom challenges and prepare to be enormously entertained!

PAPER PIG RACE

Find a friend to play with, then make two paper pigs and race each other by blowing them along! Go to www.egmont. co.uk/stampy to download a pig template!

HUNT THE CUPCAKE

Find a friend, or group of friends, and take turns hiding a cupcake for the others to find.

BOREDOM CHALLENGES

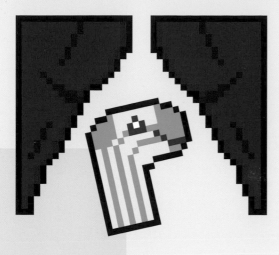

SOCK PUPPET THEATRE

Make some sock puppets and act out a play!

MY LOVELY FACE

Using only items in your house, make my face!

FAVOURITE EPISODE

Act out a play based on your favourite episode from my channel.

PLAY HIDE AND SEEK WITH ACTUAL SQAISHEY! WELL, ALMOST...

Go to www. egmont.co.uk/ stampy and download a picture of Sqaishey, then have fun hiding her around your home for your friends to find!

TOP ELEVEN MINECRAFT QUESTS

Together with my friends, I've completed so many fun quests in Minecraft and it's been really difficult to pick out my favourites. Take a journey around My Lovely World to see where each of my top eleven quests took place, then check out my channel to watch them again!

8 We battled evil clones with friendly clones in *Clone Calamity [184]*.

4 We stopped Hit The Target from blowing up my hotel with the Easter Bunny in *Egg Hunt [291]*.

1 **My Favourite Quest**
When I was ambushed in my dreams by Hit The Target in *Lovely Waterfall [62]*.

3 We put on a show in my theatre in *The Show Must Go On [69]*.

9 We had a hot air balloon battle with Hit The Target in *Fight In Flight [212]*.

2 I met Hit The Target in the Nether in *Revelation [76]*.

6 My lunar friends visit My Lovely World in their UFO in *Lunar Friends [110]*.

11 We battled Hit The Target and destroyed his castle in *Unexpected Drama [42]*.

10 I went to the moon and met my lunar friends in *Trip to the Moon [85]*.

7 We put on a big show in my circus in *The Big Show [144]*.

5 I travelled to the past in My Lovely World in *Cat to the Future [100]*.

STAMPY'S FUNLAND

PAP

MY LOVELY CAKE MAZE

Welcome to my lovely cake maze! Can you make it to the finish, collecting at least ten cakes along the way?

Colour in a cake below each time you collect a cake in the maze!

START

32

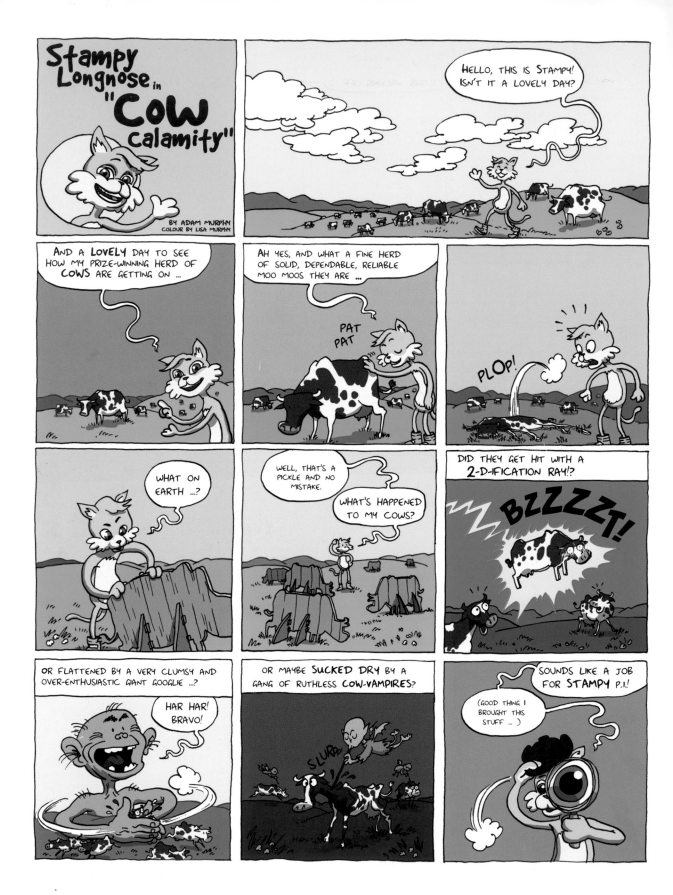

STAMPY'S HOT BUNS

I visited my favourite cake shop today, but something has changed!
Can you find five differences between these two pictures?

Colour in a cake each time you spot a difference.

ODD GOOGLIE OUT

Eek! I've wandered into a cave full of googlies! It's a googlie gathering! Can you spot the odd googlie out?

STAMPY

May all of your your cakes be tasty.

Mr Stampy Cat

SILLY SCENARIOS (WITH SQUID)

Squid and I like to play Silly Scenarios!
Find a friend and try them out for yourself!

1. Play Ice Cream Parlour with a friend. Every time the owner says the words 'ice cream', the customer has to change their mood, e.g. from excited to annoyed.

2. Act out a scene with friends. Everyone has a secret profession and you have to guess what!

3. Act out a moment from your favourite YouTube video, but swap characters every ten seconds.

5. Have a conversation with someone, but one of you can only speak in three-word sentences and the other can only speak in seven-word sentences.

6. Perform regular, everyday activities (such as making your bed) as if you are the star of a musical!

4. Have a conversation with someone without using the letter E in any of your words.

Check out my best Silly Scenarios on YouTube!
Minecraft Xbox - Quest to Kill the Wither [19]
Minecraft Xbox - Quest to Build a Beacon [113]
Minecrat Xbox - Quest For Water Park [116]
Minecraft Xbox - Quest For a Swimming Pool [117]

41

BEHIND THE SCENES

A great video doesn't just happen, it has to be planned! Here's how I plan out my videos at my drawing board.

I always follow my Five-step Process when making a Lovely World video:

1. Idea!
I'm able to come up with so many ideas because I'm always looking for inspiration. It's important to write down every idea you have as soon as you have it. You never know which ideas will turn into something really good.

2. Develop
Once I have an idea, I jump into the game and play around to see if it works. I also think about how the idea will work in a video. At this point the idea usually changes a bit.

3. Design
Once I've developed my idea, I begin designing. I construct the entire thing in a different world so I can learn how to build it and see how it looks. I also take lots of screenshots at this stage so I don't have to remember every little detail in my head!

4. Test
Once the design is finished I test what I've built. If it's a mini game I'll invite friends to play with me so I know it works and will be fun. At this point I often make some very last-minute changes.

5. Build
When I'm finally happy with everything, I gather the materials I'll need in My Lovely World and prepare an area to build on. Then I'll start recording! But I'll let you in on a secret ... I usually improvise when recording and change the design again!

NOTE
Every single thing I build in my world goes through this process!

42

MY SECRETS

Psst! **Want to know some completely confidential secrets about My Lovely World? Well, you've come to the right page!**

- My Funland used to be a lake!

- My house used to be in a desert, which is why Henry, my snow golem, didn't leave a trail of snow behind when he wandered around.

- There's a jungle biome in my world, as well as a mushroom biome. You just can't see them.

- I always record my videos in advance just in case I'm ill or can't record. Most videos were made over a month before I uploaded them to YouTube.

- When I record in My Lovely World, my helpers can all hear me, but I can't hear them.

- I make LOTS of cakes. I have so many at the moment that I could last for months without having to make any more.

- I sometimes make crazy noises right before I start recording to make me laugh and get me in a silly mood for the video.

- I secretly use items like flowers, trees or torches to mark the spot where I plan to build, so I don't get it wrong in the video.

- After I've recorded a video, I spend ages (sometimes as much as 30 minutes) taking a screenshot for the YouTube thumbnail. It is REALLY hard to get the animals to look at the camera, and I have to trick my dogs into looking at it by waving pork chops at them!

1.

Plan your videos before you start. See page 46 for a handy planning sheet template!

2.

Pick a good name and character to entertain your viewers.

3.

Make a practice video before recording the real thing and show it to family and friends before you upload.

7.

Don't get upset when things go wrong. This happens to everyone, even me!

8.

Upload videos regularly. If people love them they will want to see more.

TIPS FOR OWN VIDEO

Always ask a parent for permission before making a video and uploading to the internet, and check the minimum age for the site you want to use.

4.
Check the video is clear and that your voice can be heard.

5.
If you're really nervous, record with family and friends.

6.
Make sure you're having lots of fun. Fun times = fun videos!

9.
Don't stress about comments. You can always turn them off.

10.
Get inspired! Check out your favourite YouTubers and work out what it is that you really like about them.

VIDEO PLANNING SHEET!

CHECK BOX

1. Name yourself

2. Get inspired

3. Have a plan

4. Practice makes perfect

5. The more the merrier

6. Make yourself heard

7. Chin up

8. Keep it up

9. Ignore the meanies

10. Have fun!

46

QUIZ: WHO'S YOUR BEST FRIEND?

Sqaishey, Rosie, Amy Lee, Squid, Finnball or Hit the Target (gasp)? Take this decision tree quiz to find out which of my lovely friends you'd get on best with!

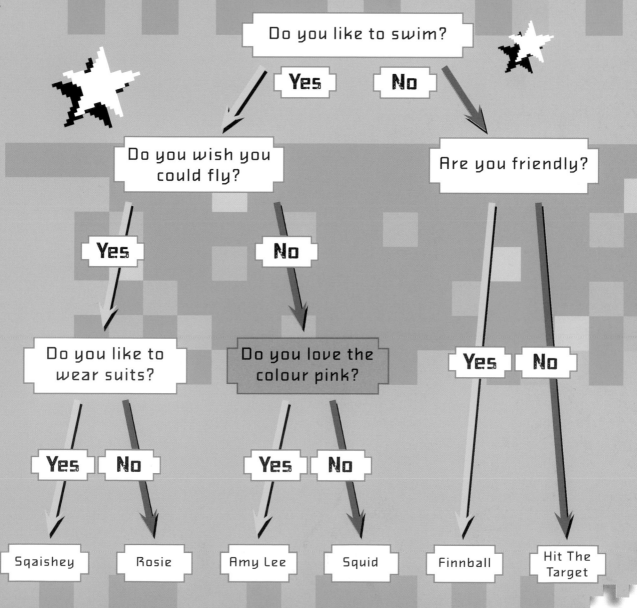

Do you like to swim?

Yes / **No**

Do you wish you could fly? — Are you friendly?

Yes / **No**

Do you like to wear suits? — Do you love the colour pink?

Yes / **No**

Yes / **No** — **Yes** / **No** — **Yes** / **No**

Sqaishey — Rosie — Amy Lee — Squid — Finnball — Hit The Target

MY SPECIAL CAKE

Everybody knows how much I love cake. I love cake so much that I've made myself a very special cake!

INGREDIENTS

Time needed: 2 hours

Cake:
[total ingredients for two layers, use half the amounts listed for each layer]
- 350g caster sugar
- 350g softened butter
- 350g self-raising flour
- 2tsp baking powder
- 6 eggs

Buttercream:
- 600g icing sugar
- 300g unsalted softened butter
- 1 teaspoon vanilla essence
- 2 tablespoons milk

Filling:
- 1 jar of strawberry jam

Fondant Icing:
- orange [small packet]
- yellow [small packet]
- black [small packet]
- green [small packet]
- white [large packet]

Equipment:
- 20 x 20 cm square cake tin
- chopping board
- rolling pin
- greaseproof paper/baking parchment
- mixing bowls
- spatula
- whisk
- cooling rack

Ask a parent or guardian to help you and a friend bake this delicious cake. Yum!

1 Sprinkle a clean chopping board with icing sugar and place a handful of each colour of fondant icing on top. Rub icing sugar onto the rolling pin and roll your icing until it's about 2 mm thick.

Cut 12 2.5 x 2.5 cm yellow squares and 24 orange squares and leave to dry. Visit www.egmont.co.uk/stampy to download a handy template to help you create my face!

2 Preheat the oven to 190°C/fan 170°C/gas 5. Cut a 20 cm square of baking paper and place it in the bottom of the first cake tin. Grease the entire tin with butter.

3 In a large bowl or mixer, beat the sugar, vanilla and butter, then gradually add the eggs. Add the flour and baking powder last and beat until the mixture is smooth. Pour into cake tin.

4 Place in your preheated oven and bake for 25 minutes. Ask an adult to test whether the cake is ready by piercing with a knife or skewer. It should come out clean.

5 Leave the cake to cool for at least 10 minutes then turn onto a cooling rack. Ask an adult to cut the edge of the cake to give it straight edges. Repeat steps 1-5 so you have 2 cake layers.

6 To make the buttercream, mix the butter and icing sugar together. Add the vanilla and mix until you have a smooth mixture.

7 Spread a third of the mixture on top of one of the cakes, then spread the jam on the other. Stack the buttercream layer on top of the jam layer.

8 Use the rest of the buttercream to cover the outside of the cake, then cover this in a layer of white fondant icing about 5 mm thick. Now you're ready to stick on my face.

9 Carefully place my face on the fondant icing. Use the orange and yellow squares to decorate the sides so that your cake looks lovely from every angle.

Ooh, that looks yummy!

How to Draw ME!

WANT TO HAVE A GO AT DRAWING ME? FOLLOW THESE INSTRUCTIONS!

1.

SINCE I'M A COMPLICATED PERSON, I CAN BE COMPLICATED TO DRAW AS WELL! THAT'S WHY I RECOMMEND DRAWING **SIMPLE SHAPES** FIRST.

IF YOU DRAW THEM **REALLY LIGHTLY** IN PENCIL, YOU CAN RUB THEM OUT LATER.

MY HEAD IS A **CIRCLE**.

MY BODY IS MORE OF A **BEAN SHAPE**.

2.

LET'S ADD BASIC SHAPES FOR MY **EYES, NOSE** AND **EARS**.

NOTICE, SINCE I'M LOOKING TO THE **LEFT** (YOUR LEFT!) MY NOSE AND EARS ARE TURNED THAT WAY.

I LIKE TO THINK ABOUT THE **CENTRE LINE** OF THE FACE TO HELP PLACE THE FEATURES.

NOTICE HOW THE EYES AND EARS ARE **EQUALLY SPACED** ON EITHER SIDE OF THIS LINE.

3.

LET'S GIVE ME **MORE DETAIL** IN MY EYES, NOSE AND MOUTH!

DRAW A CIRCLE AND A DOT IN THE MIDDLE OF MY EYES - NOW I CAN SEE!

DON'T FORGET EYEBROWS!

SINCE I'M A CAT, MY MOUTH GOES LIKE THIS.

4.

NOW LET'S ADD MY BEAUTIFUL HAIR AND WHISKERS!

NOTICE HOW MY FAR-AWAY WHISKERS LOOK SMALLER BECAUSE PARTS OF THEM ARE HIDDEN BY MY FACE!

LET'S ADD SOME EYELIDS HERE TOO.

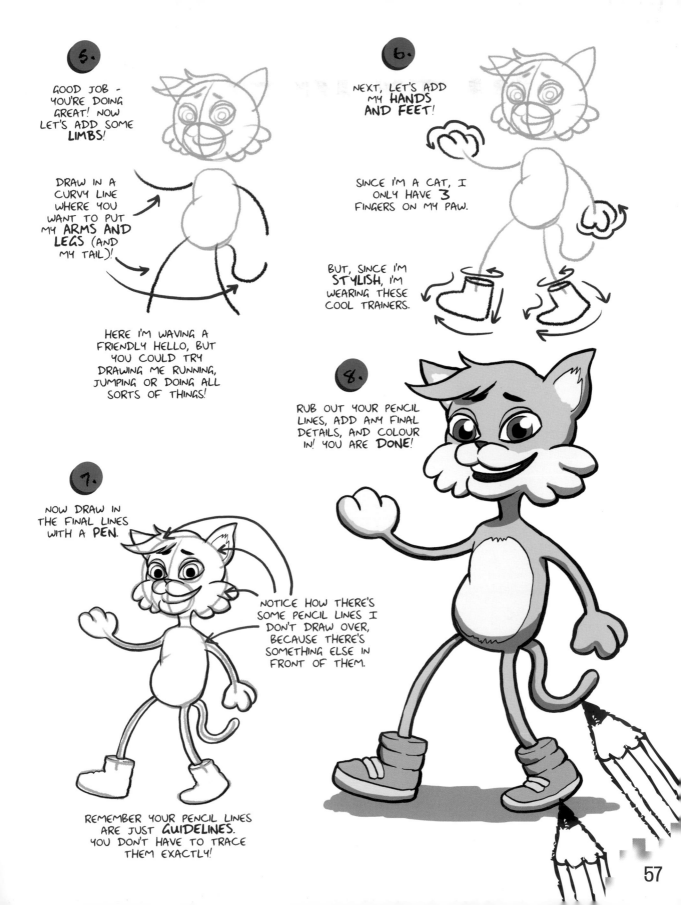

5.

GOOD JOB - YOU'RE DOING GREAT! NOW LET'S ADD SOME **LIMBS**!

DRAW IN A CURVY LINE WHERE YOU WANT TO PUT MY **ARMS AND LEGS** (AND MY TAIL)!

HERE I'M WAVING A FRIENDLY HELLO, BUT YOU COULD TRY DRAWING ME RUNNING, JUMPING OR DOING ALL SORTS OF THINGS!

6.

NEXT, LET'S ADD MY **HANDS AND FEET**!

SINCE I'M A CAT, I ONLY HAVE **3** FINGERS ON MY PAW.

BUT, SINCE I'M **STYLISH**, I'M WEARING THESE COOL TRAINERS.

8.

RUB OUT YOUR PENCIL LINES, ADD ANY FINAL DETAILS, AND COLOUR IN! YOU ARE **DONE!**

7.

NOW DRAW IN THE FINAL LINES WITH A **PEN**.

NOTICE HOW THERE'S SOME PENCIL LINES I DON'T DRAW OVER, BECAUSE THERE'S SOMETHING ELSE IN FRONT OF THEM.

REMEMBER YOUR PENCIL LINES ARE JUST **GUIDELINES**. YOU DON'T HAVE TO TRACE THEM EXACTLY!

57

BEGINNER CHALLENGE!

Whether it's your mum, a grandparent or your tech-challenged friend, it can be difficult to help beginners navigate the strange and dangerous world of gaming!

Opposite is a list of things that you might find yourself saying as you attempt to train your beginner – I definitely said lots of these to my sister Netty when I was teaching her how to play Minecraft! Some are helpful and some are not so helpful. Tick the ones you think will make your beginner feel calm and supported!

oops!

☐ You're doing great!

☐ This is so much fun!

☐ OK, but stop pressing that.

☐ Do you know how to do that? OK, I'm just going to tell you, because this is taking ages.

☐ Something just hurt you. So I'd deal with that, rather than just standing there.

☐ Do not panic!

☐ I'd recommend being quick now.

☐ Oh, no. What's happened here?

☐ I can see the situation, but not the solution.

☐ Make a conscious effort not to do that.

☐ Quick as you can! Quick as you can!

☐ How are you THIS bad?

☐ Just give me a minute to think.

☐ OK, panic time!

☐ Don't press anything!

☐ Quick quick quick quick quick!

☐ The one on the left! The one on the left! LEFT! No, not right, left!

☐ Remember: composure! Stay calm.

☐ Nooooooooooo!

☐ Gaa! I just want to grab the controller out of your hand!

nooOOO!

CAPTION THIS . . .

Hello, what's going on here? These pictures of my friends look very interesting, but I'm not sure what's happening in each one. Why don't you decide what's going on and write a caption to explain?

Caption:

Caption:

Draw something here:

60

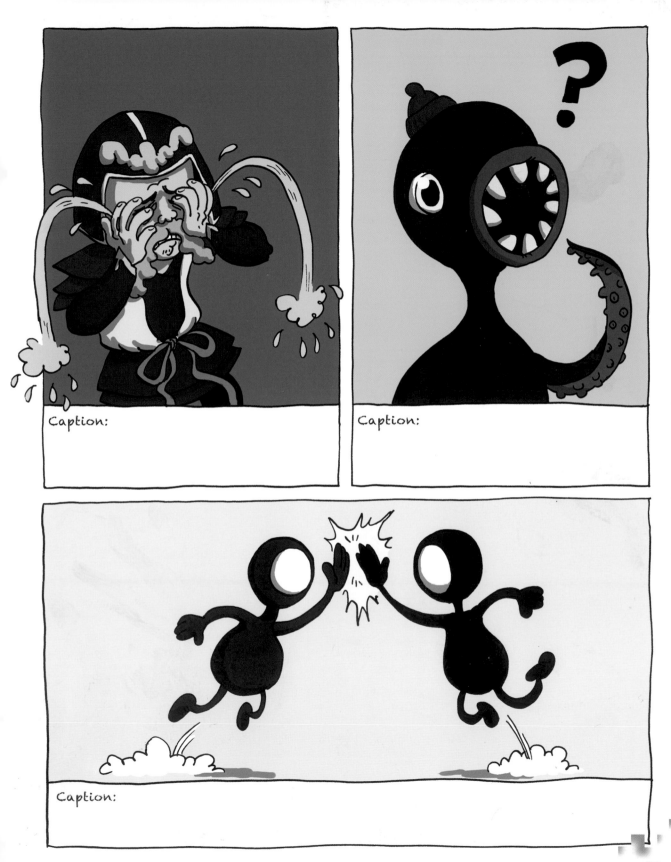

Caption:

Caption:

Caption:

WORD CHALLENGE!

Ooh, I love a good word challenge! Can you find the names of my lovely dogs in the word grid opposite? Colour in a dog bone each time you find one.

AQUA
BARNABY
BENGY
BENTON
COREY
DUNCAN
FLIPPY
FLUFFY
GREGORY JR
LUNA
SHERBET

T	G	T	F	S	H	N	A	F	J
E	J	Y	L	L	O	Y	U	L	J
B	X	R	R	T	I	B	Q	U	U
R	G	Y	N	O	E	P	A	F	J
E	K	E	M	N	G	G	P	F	V
H	B	E	G	Y	T	E	T	Y	K
S	U	Y	Y	B	A	N	R	A	B
Y	Y	E	R	O	C	N	H	G	S
D	F	S	U	E	V	Z	U	A	N
S	S	Z	U	Y	I	M	I	L	C
Q	R	J	Y	R	O	G	E	R	G
D	U	N	C	A	N	O	D	E	V

63

TEST YOUR KNOWLEDGE

So you think you're a Stampy Superfan, but how well do you really know me? Take this quiz and find out!

1. What was the name of my first dog?

....

2. What is the name of the hotel in My Lovely World?

....

3. What do I call the aliens that visit my world?

....

4. What did Santa get Harrison for Christmas?

....

5. What was the first thing I built in my Funland?

....

6. Who shot an arrow off the top of Amy Lee's head in my circus?

....

FUNLAND GAMES

Ooh, and what do we have here? Yaaaaaay!
It's my Funland, complete with mini-challenges!
Yay! Why not have a go at them?

>GOLF COURSE
• Roll up an old piece of paper into a ball.
• Put a container on the opposite side of the room.
• Find a friend and take it in turns to throw
the paper at the container. The winner
is the person who takes the fewest
throws to get it into the container.
• Alternatively, mark a spot with
an upside-down plastic cup and see
who can get their ball closest.

<FIZZ BANG
• Cut out three pieces of card and
colour them in different colours (e.g. red,
blue and green). Ask a friend to do the same.
• Take it in turns to create a sequence using
your colours and write it down (e.g. red blue
red green red blue red green).
• Show the cards to your friend in this
sequence, then ask them to repeat the
sequence back to you.
• Whoever can remember the most
sequences, wins!

>SHEEP SHUFFLE
• Put a piece of cotton wool or paper
under one of three cups.
• Shuffle the cups as fast as you
can for ten seconds while a
friend watches.
• Ask your friend to tell you which cup
is hiding the cotton wool/paper.
• Keep going until someone gets it
wrong. The other person wins!

>INVESTIGATOR

• Player One holds their hands apart at the width of their body.
• Player Two places their hands between player One's hands.
• Player One claps their hands together to try and trap Player Two's hands. Player Two must pull their hands away to avoid being trapped.
• The first person to trap the other player's hands three times, wins.

<CAT AND MOUSE

• This is just like Rock Paper Scissors, except the rock is a cat, the scissors are a mouse and the paper is cheese!

>WIGGLY WORM

• Draw a face on the end of your thumb and ask a friend to do the same.
• Let the Thumb War commence!

BYEEEEEEE!

I hope you had as much fun reading My Lovely Book as I did making it.

Thanks for reading and I'll see you later!

ANSWERS

PAGE 20-21: LOST DOGS SEARCH AND FIND

PAGE 32-33: MY LOVELY CAKE MAZE

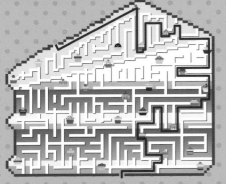

PAGE 36-37: STAMPY'S HOT BUNS SPOT THE DIFFERENCE

PAGE 38: ODD GOOGLIE OUT

PAGE 58-59: BEGINNER CHALLENGE!

You should have ticked the following:

You're doing great!

This is so much fun!

Do not panic!

Remember: composure! Stay calm.

PAGE 62-63: WORD CHALLENGE!

T	G	T	S	H	N	A	I	J	
E	J	Y	L	G	Y	U	I	I	
B	X	R	R	T	B	O	U	U	
R	G	Y	N	O	F	R	A	J	
I	K	E	M	N	G	G	P	V	
I	R	E	F	Y	T	E	T	K	
S	U	Y	Y	B	N	R	A	B	
Y	Y	E	R	G	E	N	H	G	S
D	F	S	U	E	V	Z	U	A	N
S	S	Z	U	Y	I	M	I	L	C
Q	R	J	Y	R	O	G	E	R	S
B	U	N	C	A	N	O	D	E	V

PAGE 64-65: TEST YOUR KNOWLEDGE

1. Gregory.
2. Hotel of Dreams.
3. My lunar friends.
4. A book about eyebrow grooming.
5. A golf course.
6. Ballistic Squid.

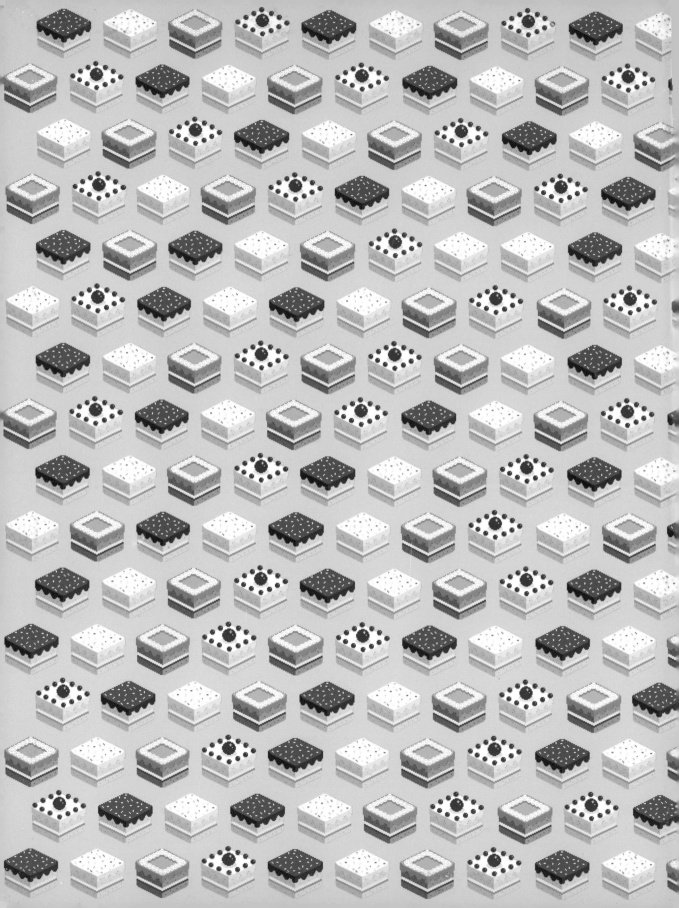